THIS WALKER BOOK BELONGS TO:

_____

_____

_____

For Sara and my mother

WALKER BOOKS
AND SUBSIDIARIES
LONDON · BOSTON · SYDNEY · AUCKLAND

First published 1991 by Walker Books Ltd,
87 Vauxhall Walk, London SE11 5HJ

This edition published 2004 for Index Books Ltd

16 18 20 19 17 15

© 1991 Kim Lewis Ltd

Printed in China

British Library Cataloguing in Publication Data:
a catalogue record for this book is
available from the British Library

ISBN 0-7445-2031-2

www.walkerbooks.co.uk

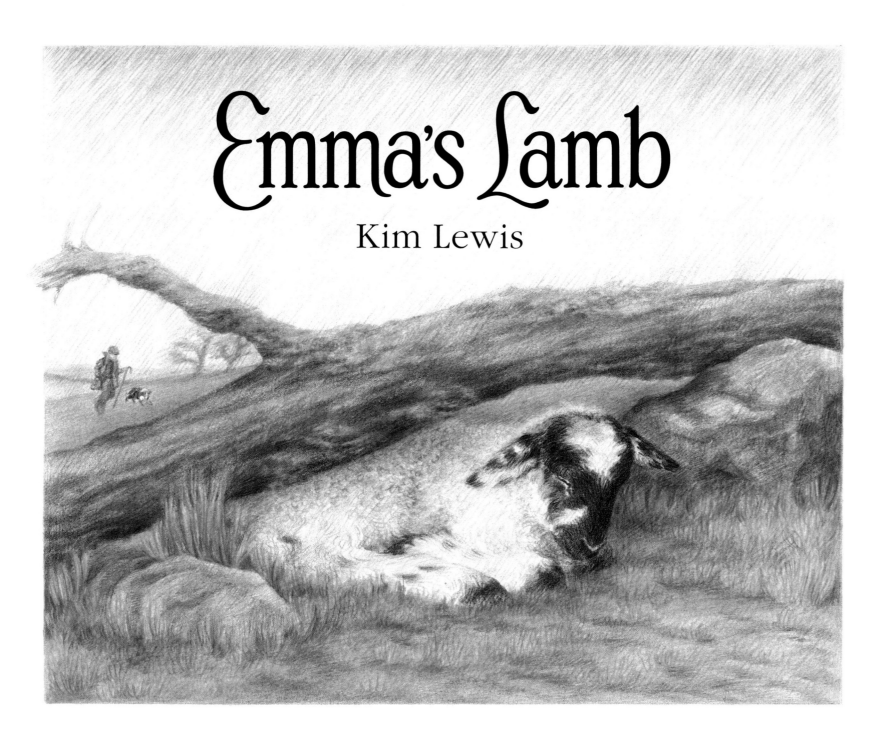

Emma's Lamb

Kim Lewis

One rainy spring morning at lambing time,
Emma's father put a little lost lamb in a box
by the stove. Then he went back
to the field to look for Lamb's mother.

Lamb and Emma looked at each other.

"Baaa," said Lamb, sitting up in his box.

Emma wanted to keep little Lamb
and look after him all by herself.

So Emma dried Lamb
because he was very wet.
She tried to keep him warm
because he was very cold.
Emma fed Lamb
because he was very hungry.

When Lamb was dry and warm and fed,
he and Emma played.
"Baaa," said Lamb, getting
into a mess.

Then Emma took Lamb for a walk
and he skipped along behind her.
Emma decided to play hide and seek.
She closed her eyes and counted to ten.
"Here I come!" she cried.

Emma looked for Lamb in the stable.

She looked for him in the barn.

She looked for him in the granary.

She looked all around the yard.

She couldn't find Lamb in the house.

He wasn't in his box.

She couldn't find him in the
sheep pens either.

"I give up!" she shouted.

But Lamb was nowhere to be found.

Emma didn't want to play any more.

She wanted Lamb to come back.

She thought he might be cold and hungry.

"Where are you, Lamb?" she cried.

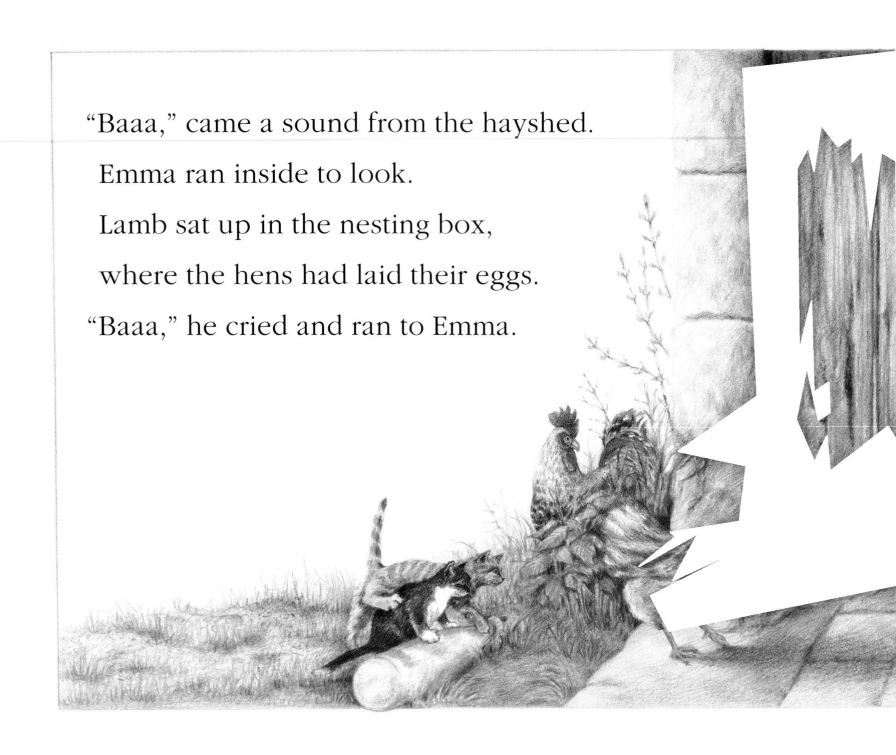

"Baaa," came a sound from the hayshed.

Emma ran inside to look.

Lamb sat up in the nesting box,

where the hens had laid their eggs.

"Baaa," he cried and ran to Emma.

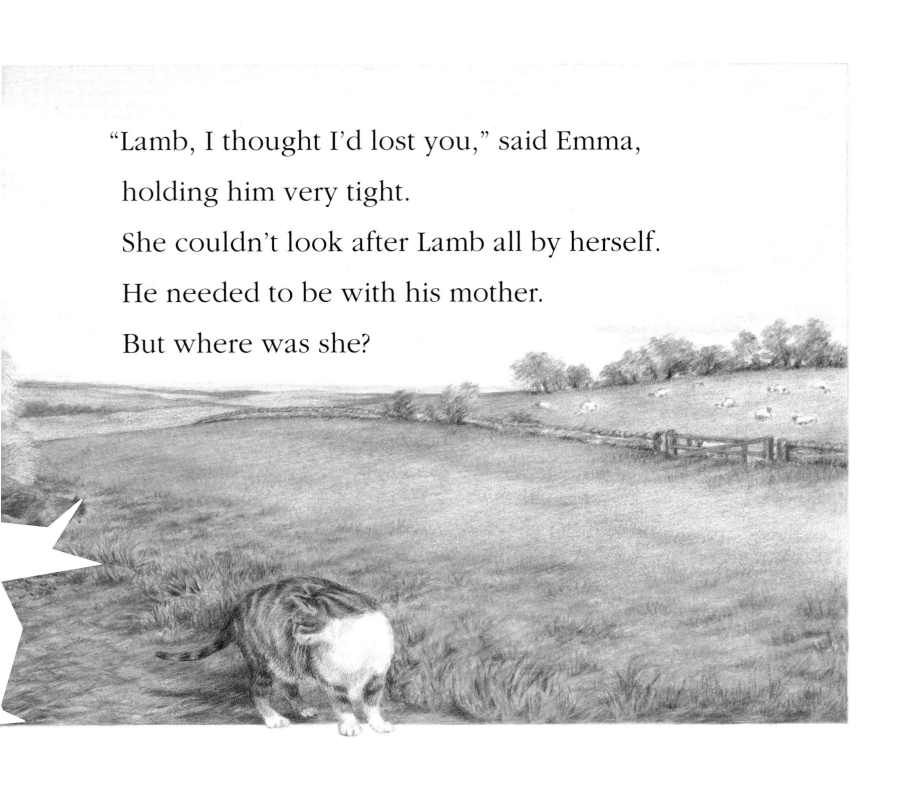

"Lamb, I thought I'd lost you," said Emma,

holding him very tight.

She couldn't look after Lamb all by herself.

He needed to be with his mother.

But where was she?

Then Emma saw her father across the field.

A ewe without a lamb ran ahead of him, calling.

"Baaa," cried Lamb. He wriggled to get free.

Emma put him down,

and Lamb ran as fast as he could to his mother.

Emma went to the field the very next day.

When she called, Lamb came running to see her.

"Will you remember me?" asked Emma.

Lamb and Emma looked at each other.

"Baaa," said Lamb, waggling his tail.

WALKER BOOKS is the world's leading independent publisher of children's books. Working with the best authors and illustrators we create books for all ages, from babies to teenagers – books your child will grow up with and always remember. So…

FOR THE BEST CHILDREN'S BOOKS, LOOK FOR THE BEAR